Chuckling Ducklings

and Baby Animal Friends

Aaron Zenz

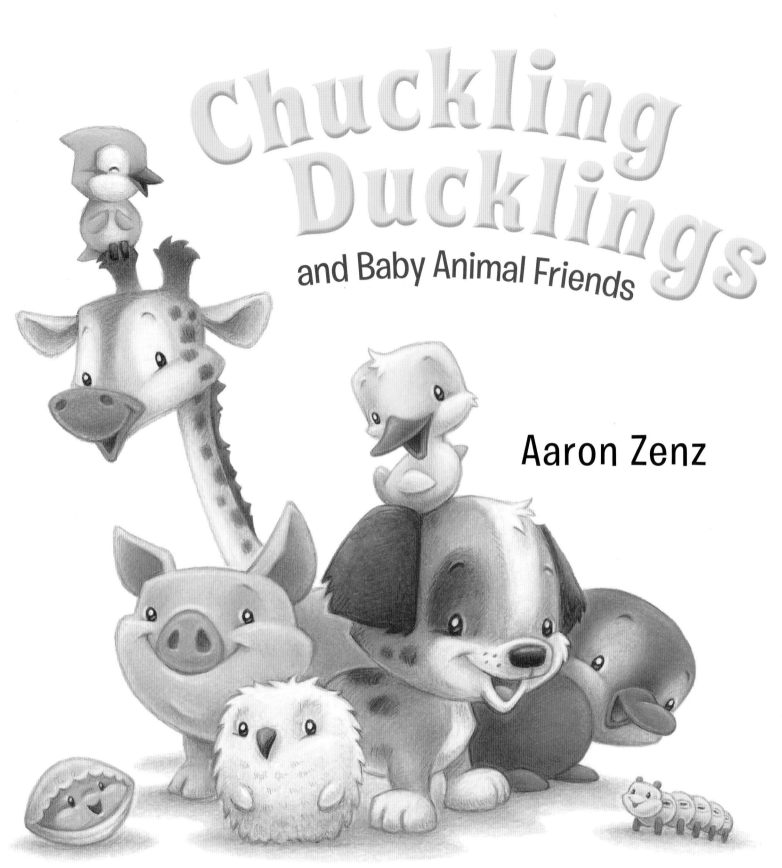

Walker & Company New York

Here's a **PUPPY**. There's a **KITTEN**.

A baby **BUNNY** is what I am.

A yawning **FAWN**

and chuckling **DUCKLINGS**.

CUB,

CUB,

CUB,

CUB,

PIGLET, LAMB.

He's a **COLT**

and she's a **FILLY**—

although both
are also
FOALS.

Butterflies were **CATERPILLARS**.

Frogs come from the wee **TADPOLES**.

OWLET,

CYGNET,

EAGLET,

EYAS,

GOSLING,

CHEEPER,

POULT, and

SQUAB.

As for all the rest of us birds,

CHICK will simply do the job.

PUGGLE? PUGGLE!

We're both **PUGGLES**.

KIT

and

PINKY,

PORCUPETTE.

What's a **CRIA**?   Who's a **JOEY**?

HATCHLINGS race the **LEVERET**.

CALVES of every shape, size, color.

I'm a **KID**. Are you one too?

PUP and **SPAT**,

WHELP and ELVER.

They call me small **FRY**.

How
about
you
?

BEAR — CUB

BLUE JAY — CHICK

BUTTERFLY — CATERPILLAR

CAMEL — CALF

DUCK — DUCKLING

EAGLE — EAGLET

ECHIDNA — PUGGLE

EEL — ELVER

ELEPHANT — CALF

GOAT — KID

GOOSE — GOSLING

HARE — LEVERET

HAWK — EYAS

MOUSE — PINKY

OSTRICH — CHICK

OTTER — WHELP

OWL — OWLET

OYSTER — SPAT

PIG — PIGLET

PIGEON — SQUAB

PLATYPUS — PUGGLE

PORCUPINE — PORCUPETTE

SHEEP — LAMB

SKUNK — KIT

SWAN — CYGNET

TIGER — CUB

TORTOISE — HATCHLING

CAT — KITTEN

CHICKEN — CHICK

COW — CALF

DEER — FAWN

DOG — PUPPY

FISH — FRY

FLAMINGO — CHICK

FROG — TADPOLE

GIRAFFE — CALF

HIPPOPOTAMUS — CALF

HORSE — FOAL

HUMMINGBIRD — CHICK

KANGAROO — JOEY

LLAMA — CRIA

PANDA — CUB

PARROT — CHICK

PELICAN — CHICK

PENGUIN — CHICK

QUAIL — CHEEPER

RABBIT — BUNNY

RACCOON — CUB

RHINOCEROS — CALF

SEAL — PUP

TURKEY — POULT

VULTURE — CHICK

WHALE — CALF

WOODPECKER — CHICK

First published in the United States of America in February 2011
by Walker Publishing Company, Inc., a division of Bloomsbury Publishing, Inc.
www.bloomsburykids.com

For information about permission to reproduce selections from this book, write to
Permissions, Walker BFYR, 175 Fifth Avenue, New York, New York 10010

Library of Congress Cataloging-in-Publication Data
Zenz, Aaron.
Chuckling ducklings / Aaron Zenz.
p.   cm.
ISBN 978-0-8027-2191-4 (hardcover) · ISBN 978-0-8027-2192-1 (reinforced)
1. Animals—Infancy—Juvenile literature. I. Title.
QL763.Z46 2011   591.3'9—dc22   2010031649

Art created with colored pencils
Typeset in Arbitrary Regular and Shag Expert Exotica
Book design by Danielle Delaney

Printed in China by Toppan Leefung Printers, Ltd., Dongguan, Guangdong
1 3 5 7 9 10 8 6 4 2 (hardcover)
1 3 5 7 9 10 8 6 4 2 (reinforced)

All papers used by Bloomsbury Publishing, Inc., are natural, recyclable products
made from wood grown in well-managed forests. The manufacturing processes
conform to the environmental regulations of the country of origin.

For my duckling, **Lily**